READ ALL OF
AXEL & BEAST'S
ADVENTURES!

For information contact:
Kane Miller, A Division of EDC Publishing
PO Box 470663
Tulsa, OK 74147-0663
www.kanemiller.com
www.edcpub.com
www.usbornebooksandmore.com

Library of Congress Control Number: 2018942398

Printed and bound in the United States of America

1 2 3 4 5 6 7 8 9 10

ISBN: 978-1-61067-851-3

AXEL & BEAST

CASTLE OF CYBORGS

ADRIAN C. BOTT ART BY ANDY ISAAC

Kane Miller

A DIVISION OF EDC PUBLISHING

This story is dedicated to Ben, whose ongoing joy and excitement at each book in the series have been the best reward any author could wish for.

CHAPTER 1

Axel Brayburn couldn't sleep.

He knew he needed rest. Tomorrow he was going on the most important mission of his life. But thinking about that mission was keeping him awake.

Over a year ago, his father, Matt, had gone to pick up some takeout for dinner and had never come home. The police had found his empty car upside down by the side of the road, without a scratch on it. None of the searches had ever turned up a single hair. Months had gone by without any news, but Axel and his mom, Nedra, had never given up hope. His dad had to be alive, somewhere.

Now Axel knew they had been right all along. His dad *was* alive – and being held prisoner by a mysterious, sinister group called the Neuron Institute. Axel had briefly met their leader, a pale man called Professor Payne who had all the charm and personality of a praying mantis.

Axel's alarm clock was a round plastic moon that lit up from within. Glowing green numbers showed the time was a minute before midnight.

Tomorrow, Axel and his shape-shifting robot friend, BEAST, would try to rescue his dad. It sounded simple when you put it like that. But Axel still didn't know what sort of enemies he was going up against, and he wouldn't know until Agent Omega arrived in the morning with the mission briefing.

He tossed and turned in the dark.

Not knowing what he was heading into was worse than knowing, somehow. His sleepy brain kept conjuring up all sorts of horrors. Professor Payne was a scientist. Maybe he made **monsters**. Perhaps there really would be **radioactive dinosaur wasps** this time. Or **shark-spider hybrids**, scuttling across the walls with mouths full of razor teeth. Maybe they would fail, and his father would never come home …

Axel rolled over and groaned into his pillow. This was like Christmas, except instead of presents, the morning would bring a surprise package full of **deadly danger**.

"AXEL?" whispered BEAST from across the room. "ARE YOU OKAY?"

"Can't sleep," Axel mumbled.

"CAN I HELP?"

"Don't know."

"SHOULD I TRY DOING THE OCEAN THING?"

"Sure. May as well."

So BEAST tried his best to sound like the sea, because that always calmed Axel down. He made the **whooshing** sounds of waves **crashing** on the shore and sometimes added the sounds of seabirds. He was careful not to do the lonely cry of a humpback whale because the one time he'd done that, it had come out louder than a car alarm and he'd woken up the entire street by mistake.

It worked. Soon Axel was snoring gently.

BEAST watched him while he slept, just in case.

The next day dawned gray and cold.

Once, Axel's secret den under the house had felt like a private fun room, somewhere to go and relax or play games with BEAST. But now, with everyone gathered around with serious faces and the most important mission of his life ahead of him, it felt more like an army command center.

Agent Omega had arrived before Axel was up. He sat on the sofa, cradling a huge mug of coffee. Beside him sat Rusty Rosie, their loyal friend, and Axel's mom. BEAST stood off to one side. He looked worried, but then, he often did.

"You ready, Axel?" Agent Omega said softly.

Axel nodded.

"Okay. We all know why we're here. This mission has only one goal. Rescue Matt Brayburn from the Neuron Institute and bring him home. Luckily, Axel and BEAST have some experience in rescuing people from **dangerous** places." Omega smiled slightly.

The Omega Operation, Axel thought. *He means the time BEAST and I tried to break him out of the Grabbem base. We barely escaped with our lives!*

"So the same steps as last time?" he asked.

"You got it. Get in, find a terminal, hack it, find out where your dad's being kept. Think of last time as a dry run."

"BEAST KNEW HIS WAY AROUND LAST TIME," said BEAST, twitching his antennae nervously.

"Good point," said Nedra. "We'd all heard of Grabbem Industries, but not these new guys.

What even *is* the Neuron Institute?"

"First, let's look at *where* they are." Omega took a device like a TV remote control from his pocket, pointed it at the table and pressed a button. A 3-D image appeared in the air before them, showing a castle perched high on a bleak mountain.

"Seriously?" Rosie said. "With a name like that I thought they'd be in some fancy science lab, not **Dracula's Castle**."

"Look closer," said Omega, and zoomed the view in. They all saw that the gloomy castle was covered with strange devices. Cables threaded up and down the walls. There were huge screens hanging over the courtyards and satellite-dish-like devices on the tower tops. The windows glowed purple and orange, and vents jetted clouds of steam out into the cold mountain air.

"The Neuron Institute specializes in one thing," he said. "Fusing man with machine. The story says they've been doing it since Victorian times, right here in the same **spooky** old castle. Some twisted freak called the Baron von Donnerstein started the trend over a hundred years ago. They've gotten much better at it since then."

"I was wrong. It's **Frankenstein**, not

Dracula," Rosie snorted. Then she saw the look on Nedra's face and said, "Oh. Sorry."

"No problem," Nedra said.

But Axel had had the same thought, and he needed to say it out loud.

"That's why they've got my dad, isn't it? They're doing experiments on him. Are they making him into a cyborg?"

"We don't know," Omega said. "And we need to find out."

"But they *could* be, right?"

"I won't lie to you. Your dad might be ... different now. You'd best be ready for anything."

"I don't care!" Nedra said savagely. "I don't care if he's changed into some ... some horrible *machine!* I just want him home where he belongs and that's what's going to happen!"

"Let's focus on the mission," Agent Omega

quickly said. "Castle Donnerstein is in eastern Zamobia, in the forest of Eisenbern. Axel, BEAST, and I will fly there in the MOT-BOL."

Axel was pretty glad about that part. The MOT-BOL might look like a **floating metal jellyfish**, but it was a comfortable way to travel.

"DO WE NEED TO FIGHT?" asked BEAST.

"Fight if you have to, but try to hide as much as you can," said Omega. "Every single person who works for the Institute is a cyborg, with built-in weapons. Then there's the **WarBorgs**, the real heavy hitters, built for the battlefield. So be careful."

"So where are they keeping my dad?" Axel asked.

"We don't know for sure," Omega admitted, "but we do know where he *isn't*. The Undercroft, the bit under the castle. Dungeons.

Abandoned cellars. Spiders the size of dinner plates. You get the gist. Seems they walled that bit off years ago and never go down there."

"Why?" asked Rosie.

"They're afraid to. There's meant to be a monster in the Undercroft. Something so horrible even Professor Payne is scared of it. Your dad's got to be in the upper section, where the labs and computer rooms are."

Everyone looked at each other in a worried way until Axel felt he had to say something. "What about apps?" Apps let BEAST change himself into different forms to do different jobs.

"I've prepared **MYTHFIRE**, **GALAHAD**, **SHADO** and a new one, **JACKHAMMER**. In case you need to do any heavy **demolition** work."

"Cool!"

"There's one more new app. It's called **PHOENIX**," said Agent Omega, but he sounded unhappy.

Axel frowned. "What's it do?"

"It's only to be used in an emergency. And you can't use it, Axel. Only BEAST can."

Axel looked at BEAST. "Tell me!"

"ONCE PHOENIX IS ACTIVATED, IT CANNOT BE STOPPED," said BEAST. "IT OVERLOADS MY CENTRAL POWER CORE AND TURNS ME INTO A BOMB."

Nedra gasped. Axel felt himself turn pale. "It's a *self-destruct*?"

"YES. BEAST WILL NOT USE IT UNLESS HE HAS TO, AXEL. TO SAVE YOUR LIFE. OR THE LIVES OF YOUR LOVED ONES."

"Don't talk like that!" Nedra yelled. "You're going to win. And you'll all come home together, safe and sound. I know you will!"

But even as she spoke, Axel seemed to feel a cold wind blowing out of the future from somewhere lonely, sad and far away. He had the strangest feeling this was going to be the last mission he and BEAST would ever go on together ...

CHAPTER 2

"GROUNDED? YOU'VE GOT TO BE KIDDING ME!"

Axel's archenemy, Gus Grabbem Junior, was red in the face. Not the jolly red of Santa's cheeks or a plump tomato, but the angry, swollen red of a **boil** about to **burst**. It made you feel that if you just pricked his nose lightly with a pin, his head would explode and plaster you from head to toe with **steaming nastiness**.

Mrs. Grabbem stood at the edge of the chaos that was Gus's room. He had spent the past ten minutes *tearing* the place apart, **flinging** piles of clothes out of drawers and **ripping** up comic books, so it was even more of a mess than usual. She stood her ground like an orange lighthouse in the face of a storm.

"It's for your own good, my treasure."

Gus picked up an electric guitar and swung it into the TV over his bed. Mrs. Grabbem flinched and shut her eyes as sparks and fragments of glass flew.

Her son dropped his arms and stood gasping for breath. Two ***wet green trails*** of snot connected his wide nostrils to his upper lip.

The Green Elevens, thought Mrs. Grabbem. *Haven't seen those in quite a few years.*

"Your father and I have discussed it and he's come around to my point of view," she said. "We can't have you racing around the world getting into trouble anymore. It's just too risky."

"THERE'S NOT A SCRATCH ON ME!" Gus howled.

Mrs. Grabbem kept her voice level. "And we

can thank our lucky stars for that. The number of vehicles you've crashed, Gussie! You could have been killed."

Gus sank to his knees and grabbed two fistfuls of his own hair. "What am I meant to do, stuck here in this place by myself? I'll go out of my *miiiiind*."

"You have plenty of toys and games to keep you amused," snapped Mrs. Grabbem, who was losing patience. "Goodness knows your father and I buy you enough stuff."

Gus looked around at his wrecked room and shrugged.

Mrs. Grabbem took that as surrender. "Good boy. Dinner's at six. I'll send someone to clear up this mess."

"Guess I'll see you at six, then," Gus muttered. "Unless you want to come up and yell at me some more."

"That will do," Mrs. Grabbem said firmly, and shut the door.

Left alone in the chaos of his room, Gus felt strange. He didn't even want to break anything anymore. He realized he felt sorry for himself, and couldn't understand why. The answer was floating just out of reach – if he could only grasp it.

He *did* have a lot of stuff. His mom and dad were unthinkably rich – multi-multi-billionaires who could have anything they wanted. And they had bought him a spectacular number of presents. He had a game collection that would be the envy of any kid on the planet. So why, Gus wondered, did he feel so empty inside?

He thought of Axel, and his eyes narrowed. Maybe that was what he needed to focus on. **Revenge.** After all, it was Axel's fault that he was grounded. Hadn't it been Axel and his stolen BEAST robot that had kept wrecking his plans?

Yes. That had to be it. He grinned a wicked grin at the thought of *ripping* BEAST's arms and legs off and making Axel watch. The more Axel cried, the more fun it would be. It would be even better than all the times he'd beaten Axel in *Tankinator Arena,* the online game they both played. Axel had been AX-MAN, and he'd been BAGGER_63. Maybe he should remind Axel of that, rub his nose in it some more.

But how? He was still grounded! He clenched his fist.

If only there was some way he could hunt Axel down without ever leaving the mansion. Some remote-controlled device, maybe. Or a **hunter-killer drone**. Or a super-powered clone of himself …

An idea hit him like a lightning bolt. For

a second he stood speechless, amazed at his own brilliance.

"Oh, man," he said to himself. "I'm a genius."

And he went bounding out of his room. He sprinted to the elevator at the end of the corridor. Buttons offered a choice of any floor he might wish to travel to in the huge underground factory complex that lay below the Grabbem mansion. He slid the whole button panel upward, found the secret control for the **Experimental Projects** level, and pressed it.

As the son of the company's owners, Gus had a special platinum key card. It could get him into any room in the entire place, no matter how secret.

Or how dangerous.

The sign on the door read **TOP SECRET – AUTHORIZED PERSONS ONLY!**

Gus clicked his key card into the slot and the door slid open with a sinister hiss.

The lab beyond was dark. Only the cool blue light of the computer screens showed the outlines of furniture in the room. From the far end came a different kind of light, a bubbling frenzy of ripples. *That must be the Operating Tank*, Gus thought.

He felt a **wild excitement** to be doing this forbidden thing. Of all the Grabbem projects he'd ever heard of, this was by far the most expensive. He'd never be trusted with it normally. If his parents found out he'd borrowed it, he wouldn't just be grounded. He'd be disowned – sent to a military boarding school, probably.

"Come on, come on," he whispered. "Where is it?"

He crept farther into the back of the lab and turned a corner. A shape loomed out of the darkness. Before he could stop himself, Gus let out a **terrified** little squeal, the sort a piglet might make if it had just jumped out of a plane and realized it had left its parachute behind.

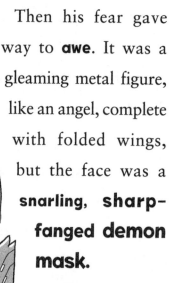

Then his fear gave way to **awe**. It was a gleaming metal figure, like an angel, complete with folded wings, but the face was a **snarling, sharp-fanged demon mask.**

Whoever had designed this thing

had meant to strike terror into the heart of its enemies.

Out of sheer bravado, Gus grasped it by its cold metal hand. "Why hello there, Project TT-93. I understand you're called the **Titanium Terror**."

The angel didn't respond.

Gus turned his attention to the luminous, bubbling cylinder nearby. *The Operating Tank.* He thought back to his father's last-but-one Big Tour, when he'd been showing his allies around the base:

"This is a highly sensitive project for us," his father had said. *"It's our first dip into virtual reality. Imagine you need to send someone to do an important job, but you can't risk sending a human because they might get injured. So you send a robot, right? But robots aren't smart like humans. They can't*

think on their feet. What you need is a human mind in a robot body! And that's what we've got here. The pilot climbs into the Operating Tank, and the clever little computers send his nerve signals through to the robotic angel. Ta-daaah! You get to become an indestructible robot warrior without leaving the safety of the lab! Then, when the mission's over, you just disconnect and go have a shower. Job done."

Shaking with excitement, Gus stripped down to his grubby underpants. He climbed up the ladder and lowered himself into the Operating Tank. The fluid wasn't even cold like he'd expected. An oxygen mask clamped onto his face.

"Please hold still," crooned a computer voice. "Scanning nerve signals."

Gus felt a tingle all over. He closed his eyes ...

… and opened them.

He was looking through robot eyes. He saw a doughy, pale boy floating in a tank. *That's me,* he thought. He looked down at his robot body and flexed his robot hands.

"I can fly," he said, and the harsh electronic voice that came out of his mouth startled him. "I can fire energy beams. I can drop bombs. And I can't be killed. Guess what, Axel. I'm coming for you!"

CHAPTER 3

"ARE YOU ALL RIGHT, AXEL?" said BEAST.

"Huh?" Axel, who had been looking out of the MOT-BOL window for the past few hours, snapped back to attention.

"YOU ARE VERY QUIET. ARE YOU MEDITATING BEFORE WE GO INTO BATTLE?"

Axel shook his head. "I was just thinking

about everything that's happened since you came to our house that day, all those weeks ago. It's been crazy. Going on missions, getting into **danger**. But I've loved it."

"BEAST LOVED IT TOO. WHATEVER HAPPENS, WE WILL ALWAYS HAVE THE GOOD TIMES."

"Don't you two go soft on me, now," said Omega. "We've got a fight coming, and we all need to be on top of our game. Stay focused on the here and now, and trust one another. You with me?"

Axel nodded. "I'm with you."

"Good man. We'll reach the Forest of Eisenbern in ten minutes. **Stay alert.**"

The MOT-BOL whirred through the sky at maximum speed. Soon they passed above a mountain range sprinkled with frost and snow, surrounded by a blanket of dark-green forest

that looked like moss from so high up.

"There's the castle!" Axel said. "What are those metal things on the turrets? They look like satellite dishes."

Omega frowned. "Scanners, probably."

"They're turning. Pointing at us. Maybe they're some kind of scientific –"

"Incoming fire!" Omega yelled.

From the tips of the "scanners" came thumping blasts of solid light that lit up the mountainside with unearthly colors. Agent Omega heaved at the controls, but the MOT-BOL hadn't been built for combat and it steered like a brick. One of the blasts fizzed overhead, but the rest slammed home.

Axel dived away from the window just as a deafening **shrannggg** tore through the craft.

All the lights went off, then back on, but

flickering. Axel smelled smoke. Cold, fresh air blew in his face. How was that possible? He was inside the MOT-BOL and its windows didn't open …

Then he saw the holes in the hull. Holes so big you could drive a truck through them.

Axel thought: *Those blasts punched right through and out the other side!*

BEAST was still locked in place in the middle of the craft. His eyes were wide with fear.

"We're going down!" Agent Omega screamed.

Axel had never been sure what sort of mysterious antigravity engines kept the MOT-BOL up in the sky, but one thing was for sure. They weren't working anymore.

Wind whistled up and around Axel as the craft **plunged toward** the waiting mountains.

Omega grabbed Axel's shoulder. "Get into BEAST and get out of here while you've got a chance!"

"But what about you?"

"Going to **crash-land** if I can. This old meatball's tougher than it looks. Go!"

Axel pulled open BEAST's canopy, climbed in and thumped the release control. They went into free fall for a second, then BEAST's foot rockets fired and they shot off through the sky, away from the doomed MOT-BOL. It fell like a meteor, trailing smoke behind it.

Axel tried to get his bearings. The turrets were still blazing away, filling the air with torpedo-sized pulses of energy.

He and BEAST rocketed toward the castle

walls. What an ugly building it was! It was like a great stone vegetable that had sprouted in the dark. He didn't want to think of the experiments that must be going on inside. Maybe there really was a monster down in the dungeons. *Merging man with machine ...* But his dad was in there too, somewhere. And Axel needed to find him.

Axel shook himself, trying to focus. "BEAST, scan for a way in," he said.

"MAIN GATEWAY IS DEFENDED BY TURRETS," BEAST said. "NO OTHER ENTRANCES FOUND."

"Guess we'll just have to make one, then." Axel scanned the wall for its weakest spot. "There! Land and shift into **JACKHAMMER** form."

From somewhere in the distance came a dull **ker-thoom**. The MOT-BOL had crashed to the ground. Axel prayed Agent Omega was still alive.

BEAST shifted. A thick metal dome covered his head, like a construction worker's helmet. His right fist thickened and became a hammer. His left fist folded away and a whizzing drill slid out of his arm.

With a yell, Axel shoved the drill deep into the castle wall, hoping to weaken it. A spray of dust and stone chips blasted out. He bored two more holes, then swung the hammer.

JACKHAMMER packed a punch, all right. The whole wall shuddered. A hideous gargoyle that had squatted in place for five hundred years broke off and smashed to bits on the ground below.

Axel swung another blow and this time, the ancient blocks gave way. Through clouds of dust, Axel saw they'd opened up a hole that might be wide enough to clamber through.

He started toward it – and a terrible **howl**

echoed across the landscape.

It was a howl to freeze the blood. It was like the cry of a **hungry wolf**, but *metallic* somehow, like the twanging of a giant steel spring.

"INCOMING LIFE FORM," BEAST warned.

"I see it!" Axel gulped.

The creature came creeping through the

forest, its red eyes glowing.

It had been a wolf, once. It still had the shape of that wild animal, and BEAST could hear its savage heart thumping. But its body was covered with metal as well as fur, and the teeth it bared were sharp shards of steel.

Cyberwolf!

CHAPTER 4

The cyberwolf slipped between the thick pine trunks, keeping to the shadows, its eyes shining as bright as hot coals. It moved slowly, but showed no fear at all.

"It's getting ready to attack," Axel said.

He glanced at the hole in the wall. It *might* be big enough to squeeze through, but what if it wasn't? He imagined BEAST stuck halfway. The cyberwolf would sink its metal razor teeth into BEAST's legs and drag him out. Then, when he was helpless on his back in the snow, it would tear him to pieces.

No way would Axel let that happen. JACKHAMMER wasn't supposed to be a combat form, but a hammer was still a hammer and a drill was a drill. He glared at the cyberwolf and swung the hammer down to strike the ground – **thoooom**.

"Come on!" he yelled.

The cyberwolf hesitated. Then it gave a steely growl, answering Axel's challenge. It padded out from the forest, letting Axel see it clearly. Slowly, it bared its **massive steel teeth** and licked its lips with a shiny snake-like tongue. At the tongue's tip was a lethal-looking spike.

It wants me to be afraid, Axel thought. *And I AM afraid. But I'm not going to show it.*

"What are you supposed to be?" Axel mocked. "Part dog, part trash can?"

The cyberwolf showed no sign of understanding. It kept coming, slowly and purposefully.

Axel watched it closely, ready for the moment it would break into a charge.

Pad, pad, pad.

Any second now.

Pad, pad, pad.

Come on, attack! What are you waiting for?

Like lightning the thought **flashed** across Axel's brain: This thing *wants* me to keep watching it! Because while I'm looking one way, something else must be sneaking up on me!

Axel spun around. He saw two more cyberwolves – lean, fast-moving brutes – only feet away. They leaped.

BEAST's hammer slammed down on one

of them, hard and heavy. It went skidding sideways across the snow, **yelping** in a high-pitched screech. The other wolf caught hold of BEAST's shoulder and ripped a piece of armor plating clean off.

Axel whacked it. There was a *skree* of grinding metal and the cyberwolf's eyes flickered. It fell back and landed with a sound like a bag of coins.

Axel turned back to face the first cyberwolf. It paced back and forth and glared at him hatefully.

"Did I spoil your surprise?" Axel taunted.

The wolf **howled** and **howled** again. At first Axel thought it was just angry, but then he realized it was a summoning howl. More cyberwolves emerged from the forest – nine, ten, *eleven* of them – and each one looked just as mean as the first!

Axel backed BEAST up against the wall, so at least he couldn't be attacked from behind.

The wolves grinned and stalked across the snow toward them.

BEAST moaned, "THERE ARE TOO MANY, AXEL!"

He's right, Axel thought. *We can't win this! They'll keep coming until BEAST's torn to bits. How am I meant to fight these things? Even if we shift to a fighting form like GALAHAD, we're still outnumbered!*

Maybe fighting the wolves hand to hand was wrong. Maybe he could fight their *minds* somehow. After all, despite their cyborg bodies, they were still animals. What were wolves afraid of?

"BEAST, go into **MYTHFIRE** form, as fast as you can!"

BEAST *shifted.*

The wolves fell back and circled warily. What was this new trick?

BEAST fell forward as his arms and legs turned into the clawed limbs of his **dragon** form. Smoke rose from his mouth, which grew into a long snout.

Axel let loose the biggest fire blast he could summon – not at the wolves, but into the air above them. A huge ball of fire **bloomed** out, bathing the mountainside in angry light.

All the wolves instantly went into a wild panic. They turned and ran, howling in fear. Axel sent a few more blasts of flame after them, just to speed them up a bit.

"It worked! The fire drove them away!"

Time to move. He shifted BEAST into his regular form, then squeezed through the hole in the wall and into the dark hallway beyond.

"I'm coming, Dad," he whispered.

"Wherever you are, hang in there. I'm not leaving without you."

They crept through a warren of wood-paneled corridors, hunting for a computer terminal. Tiny cleaning robots **buzzed** back and forth on the flagstone floors, paying no attention to them – at least, Axel hoped they weren't.

Eventually they found their way into a grand hall, like a cross between a wicked baron's home and a mad scientist's lair. A black marble-topped dining table, engraved with a circuit-board design, almost filled the room. Suits of armor stood by the doors, but the helmets' eye slits glowed red, shining out scanning beams that tracked back and forth. There were animal heads mounted on the walls, but they all had robotic parts.

The open fireplace was the largest Axel had ever seen, big enough to roast an ox in. It too was a mix of ancient and futuristic parts. BEAST's display told Axel that the bricks were centuries old, but the flames that danced in the hearth were holograms projected from beneath.

"This place is *weird*," Axel said. "But at least we made it inside. Right?"

But the far door **crashed** open before they could take another step.

There stood Professor Payne, the overseer of the Neuron Institute. Men in black suits and sunglasses, with leather gloves and stern faces, filed past him and into the room. They stood pointing their fingers at Axel as if they were guns.

Then something tall and silvery stalked in, and Axel felt a fear grip him unlike anything

he'd felt before. It was a **robotic angel** with a snarling, fanged face like a vampire. There was no mercy in those blank oval eyes.

"I suggest you take a seat, young man," said Professor Payne. "Make yourself comfortable. After all, you're not going anywhere."

CHAPTER 5

Axel remembered Professor Payne clearly from the last time they'd met. Mr. Grabbem had been showing some powerful people around his factory, and Payne had been one of them: a stiff, unsmiling man who looked about as healthy as a waxwork. He had the glassy, dead eyes of a stuffed animal. Axel was sure that his skin must be some kind of rubber, with circuits and sliding pistons underneath.

The Neuron Institute agents kept their fingers pointed at him. BEAST's display read **ROBOTIC HANDS - POWERFUL CRUSHING GRIP - ARMOR-PIERCING DART FINGERS**.

Armor-piercing darts? Suddenly Axel didn't feel so safe inside BEAST's heavily armored body.

He scanned the robotic angel next, and almost gasped aloud. It was a **walking weapons factory** – laser cannon, smart bombs, even a tractor beam to drag targets toward it. How could they stand a chance against something that powerful?

We'd have been safer out among the cyberwolves, he thought.

"Come, come," said Professor Payne irritably. "You are not an ignorant boy. You can see you are outnumbered and outgunned. Yes?"

"Looks that way," said Axel.

"Very good. There is only one logical thing for you to do, then. You will do exactly as you are told, or we will **destroy** you and your robot. Is that clear?"

Axel hesitated. Something didn't add up.

There were a lot of weapons pointed at him. Easily enough to destroy them. In fact, there were far *more* than enough.

Weird. Why would a logical, efficient man like the professor bring many times more weapons than he needed? It would be like taking out a tank with an atom bomb.

In an instant, Axel had it: *Because it's a bluff! He isn't planning to destroy us right away – he just wants me to think he will!*

Axel took a deep breath. He said, "No."

"What?"

"No. Because I don't believe you, professor."

The professor blinked and swallowed. His eyes seemed to move back into his skull for a second, like a frog's. "Explain yourself."

"You aren't going to destroy us. Not yet. You *need* something from us. Or we wouldn't be talking like this. You would have **blasted** us already."

"JUST SHOOT THEM!" rasped the robotic angel. "DON'T YOU KNOW WHO THEY ARE? THAT'S AXEL AND BEAST!"

Axel felt a nasty shock as the robotic angel said his name. How did it know who they were?

Professor Payne held up a warning finger. "I shall say this only once. Grabbem are welcome here, even when they visit unexpectedly. But I do *not* take orders from them."

So, the angel was from *Grabbem*! That explained how it knew who Axel and BEAST were. But what was it doing here? Was it some new kind of **battle robot**? And why did it sound so … lifelike? Its voice had been full of a very human anger, but Axel couldn't see any human parts. It didn't make sense.

The angel folded its arms. "WHATEVER," it said.

The professor smiled, but you could tell he wasn't used to it, because it looked like a gash slowly appearing in a fatty piece of ham. "At ease, gentlemen," he said to the agents. "The boy has bravely stood his ground, and for that he has earned my respect."

The agents withdrew their pointing gun fingers and stood with their arms folded behind their backs. The robotic angel made a disgusted "tchah" sound and leaned against the wall to watch what was coming next.

Axel let himself relax, but not too much. He'd bought himself some time. Now he had to find a way out of here and track down his dad. All the doors were blocked by agents, so he'd have to find another route. One they wouldn't have thought of.

Secretly, he typed a message so only BEAST could see it: **Where does that fireplace lead to?**

Instantly, faint blue lines appeared on BEAST's screen, showing – as if in X-ray – the shape of the chimney beyond. It was wider than Axel had dared to hope. The only question was, would it be wide enough?

The professor took a seat opposite Axel and studied him carefully. "You are correct, Axel. I do want something from you. I need to *study* you. The way you and that robot work together is phenomenal. We could learn a great deal."

"Why would I help someone like you?" Axel scoffed.

"Ah. You think me a simple **villain**, I

see. Someone who turns living beings into **cyborg monsters**, purely for the fun of it."

"Sounds about right."

"Then tell me this," said the professor. "In all your days of fighting against Grabbem Industries, have you ever asked yourself what will happen when they win?"

"They won't!"

"Oh, but they will," Professor Payne said. "Grabbem are too strong to be stopped now. They will take over more and more of the planet: **conquering, plundering** and **ravaging** everything in their path. They will leave it **scarred** and **burned**, stripped of its natural resources. A wasteland. And what manner of creatures do you suppose will survive, when this planet becomes a waking nightmare?"

Axel thought back to the cyberwolves. He imagined a world turned into a red desert, the skies smoky with pollution. Barely any food. Almost no water. A human who could survive that would have to be tough, specially adapted. Maybe it would have a breathing mask instead of a mouth. And cyborg eyes instead of fragile, human eyes ...

"So that's it," he said in a hollow voice. He remembered his mom's fear – that his dad would have become some horrible machine – and **shuddered**.

"I see you understand our work now," replied the professor. "We are preparing a new breed of beings – humans and animals made strong with technology. Strong enough to rule over a ruined world!"

BEAST didn't dare to speak out loud. Instead he flashed up a message on his internal screen:

AXEL STOP THEM AXEL PLEASE.

"Is that what you've done with my father?" Axel demanded.

The robotic angel jerked to attention. "FATHER?" it said. It didn't sound mocking or cruel. It just sounded surprised.

The professor steepled his fingers. "And now we get to the point of your little visit. No, Axel. Your father is not being prepared for the world to come. He is part of a far more exciting experiment, in the **Tower of the Living Computer!**"

Axel was trembling. "Take me to him *now*, or I promise I'll bring this whole filthy castle down around your ears!"

The agents surrounding Axel whipped their fingers up to point at him once again.

"Don't bother with the threats," said Professor Payne coolly. "One more outburst like that and I just might give you to our Grabbem friend here."

The robotic angel punched a fist into its open palm.

Axel had heard enough. He started to walk, slowly, around the great table. The fireplace, with its holographic fire, was only a few feet away. The agents' fingers followed him as he moved.

"Take me to my dad," he said.

"Not until you agree to give me what I want," said the professor.

Axel reached the fireplace. It was so huge that you could have driven a truck into it. He stood with his back to the dancing, heatless flames.

"So, you want to know the secret of how BEAST and I work together?" he said.

The professor craned forward. "Tell me."

"We're *friends*, you jerk," Axel said. "That's all. There's no secret."

"Ah." The professor's face fell. "I was mistaken, then. You have no value to me at all. Agents? **Blast them.**"

This was the moment Axel had waited for. As the agents opened fire, he quickly dived away from the hail of darts and into the fireplace. The chimney shaft gaped above him.

"Bye!" he said, and gave a little wave.

"NO!" screamed the angel.

Axel fired BEAST's foot rockets. Like Santa in reverse, they shot up the chimney. The sounds of yelling and gunfire echoed all around them as they rushed on into the darkness …

CHAPTER 6

The chimney walls were black with the soot of centuries and crisscrossed with hanging cobwebs. They looked so crumbly that Axel was scared they might cause a cave-in. He flew BEAST carefully up the very center of the chimney shaft, missing the edges by a hair's breadth.

As soon as he could be sure they were out of danger – for now, at least – Axel slowed down.

"We have to find the **Tower of the Living Computer**," he said. "If we keep going up, we'll come out the top of the chimney. The turrets will shoot at us, but we might be able to dodge ..."

"AXEL, ARE WE GOING UP?" said BEAST.

"Yeah. Well done back there, by the way. You did great."

"THANK YOU, AXEL. SO DID YOU. AND WE HAVE TO GO DOWN."

"What? We can't. Dad's in a *tower*, not a dungeon!"

"I THINK WE SHOULD GO DOWN. A LONG WAY DOWN. RIGHT THROUGH THE FLOOR AND KEEP GOING, THROUGH ALL THE CELLARS AND INTO THE UNDERCROFT."

Axel let out an exasperated sigh. "Have you got a loose wire in your head or something?

Why would we go *down?* Omega said even the Institute guys don't go under the castle. The monster, remember?"

Axel felt BEAST shudder. "I REMEMBER. AND I AM SCARED. BUT WE NEED TO FIND THE MONSTER."

"Find it? Why?"

"BECAUSE THE BAD MEN ARE AFRAID OF IT. AND BEAST THINKS SOMETIMES MONSTERS ARE NOT WHAT THEY SEEM."

Axel closed his eyes. This was just too frustrating. Why, of all the times when he could have malfunctioned, was BEAST blowing a fuse *now?*

Chasing after monsters sounds crazy, he thought. *And down has to be the wrong way to go. But... I do trust BEAST. And he needs to know I trust him.*

"Okay, then. Down it is. If we hit the floor hard enough we should **smash** clean through."

There was no way to turn around in the cramped chimney, so Axel reluctantly switched BEAST's foot rockets off. They fell like a plummeting elevator.

"Oh, man. Here we go …"

From below came the dull **whump** of an explosion. Axel looked down and saw a wall of flame rushing up the chimney toward them.

"Payne's trying to blast us out!" he yelled. "BEAST, we can't keep going. We have to turn back!"

"AXEL, PLEASE!"

Axel reached for the throttle control. He squeezed, but nothing happened. For the first time ever, BEAST had overridden his own control systems.

"We're going to die," Axel said.

And they plunged into the heart of the furnace.

There was a deafening **thra-koom** as more explosions went off, right next to them. BEAST's body shuddered as they smashed through the fireplace floor. Bricks rained down on them, blown loose by the force of the blast. Then they were free-falling, tumbling over and over.

Axel didn't even feel the impact when they crashed down on a flagstone floor hundreds of feet below. He had already passed out.

There was a cold breeze blowing on Axel's face. He could smell the damp mineral smells of old stonework and mossy cobbles, like a pavement after the rain. From somewhere nearby came the drip of falling water.

Something was wrong. It took him a second to work out what it was.

I'm not inside BEAST anymore!

Total darkness surrounded him. He forced himself to stay calm. What had happened? Oh, yes – the falling, and the **explosions**. He must have been thrown out of BEAST when the robot hit the floor.

But how? Axel wondered groggily. *I was wearing my safety harness like I always do.*

He sat up, wincing at the fresh bruises on his arms and legs. Then he froze. There was a new sound approaching, a dragging, harsh sound of metal scraping on stone.

Footsteps.

A dim, flickering light came into the room. It lit up the archway that the oncoming *thing* was passing through.

Axel didn't move as it trudged into the room. It must have been human at some stage, but you could hardly call it human anymore. A stooping, ogre-like form, it **wheezed** and **clunked** with every step. There were riveted plates all over its body and pipes sprouting from its flesh. A dull light shone from its chest, flickering blue like an old gas flame.

The monster. It's real.

It crossed the flagstones until it reached a heap of metal in the middle of the room. Then it shook its head and made a sad sound. With one paw-like hand it reached up and unplugged a cable from its body. Electric sparks fizzled.

Axel almost sobbed out loud. That wasn't a heap of metal. It was BEAST – what was left of him after the fall. And this inhuman *thing* was going to drain BEAST's last spark of energy, or maybe break him up for scrap.

No matter how frightened Axel was, he couldn't let that happen. He knew he was face-to-face with the monster of the Undercroft, but as Rosie had once told him, "If you can't be brave, then be **angry** instead – it'll serve you just as well in a pinch."

"Leave him alone!" he yelled.

The creature started in surprise. It turned to look at Axel.

The face *was* human. He could see that now. It might have **metal ribs** bulging from the forehead and a coppery stub where the chin should be, but it was still a person. Or had been, once.

"Oh no," Axel said, feeling faint. "It can't be you."

"Hnnn?" said the creature.

"Is that ... is that you, Dad?"

CHAPTER 7

The creature's face broke into a big, kindly grin. "Oh, no, young man. I am *not* your father."

Axel hesitated, taken aback by how well-spoken the creature was.

"Are you the monster, then?"

"Monster?" It chuckled, and the sound was like the **wheezing whumps** of a car trying to start on a cold morning. "*They* think so. Those fools in the upper castle. But then, I think of *them* as monsters."

It took a step forward. Axel flinched, and then felt bad about it. The creature might *look* scary, but it wasn't *acting* scary.

"Please do not be afraid," the "monster" said.

Axel swallowed his fear as best he could, strode over and held out his hand. "Axel Brayburn. Pleasure to meet you."

Delighted, the creature took his hand in his huge, misshapen claw. "Likewise! I am called Gustav. But you probably know me as the **Baron von Donnerstein**."

Agent Omega's words flashed into Axel's mind. *"Fusing man with machine. Some twisted freak called the Baron von Donnerstein started the trend a hundred years ago …"*

"THE Baron?" he said in awe. "The original? So you're what … a hundred years old?"

"One hundred and sixty-three," said the Baron, turning his attention back to BEAST. "When my body parts wear out, I can simply replace them. That is the advantage of being mostly mechanical. So, Axel, why have you come to this terrible place?"

"I'm trying to find my father and bring him home. He's a prisoner here."

"I see," rumbled the Baron. "Now, whatever happened to your poor companion?"

BEAST was in a terrible state. His power was off, and one of his arms had been **wrenched** out of his body. Axel had never seen him so bad.

"He wouldn't listen to me," he said, feeling bitter and sad and angry all at once.

"Hmm. Let me see now. Perhaps a little boost would help." The Baron found BEAST's power socket and plugged the cable from his own body into it. Immediately, BEAST's eyes lit up.

"Luckily, I have energy to spare," the Baron explained.

Axel ran to his friend's side. "BEAST, are you okay? Can you hear me?"

BEAST's voice was weak. "AXEL? DID WE FIND THE MONSTER?"

Axel looked up at the Baron. "Yes. And you were right. He isn't what he seems."

Gus Grabbem Junior was getting angry again. He waved the robotic angel's gun arm in Professor Payne's face.

"I'm telling you, you need to send a squad down there after him!"

The professor glanced at the collapsed ruin of the fireplace, where Gus had thrown half-a-dozen bombs. "Unthinkable," he said.

"He's still alive down there. And if you won't go get him then I will."

"Do so at your own risk, fool!" hissed the professor.

The Baron's rooms were surprisingly comfortable, as far as stone cells under ancient castles went. Axel sat on a sofa sipping tea, while BEAST patiently waited for the Baron to finish welding his arm back on.

"Why is the Neuron Institute so scared of you?" Axel asked.

"Probably because every time I escape from these dungeons, I smash up their laboratories in a **berserk rage** until they knock me out and throw me back down here again," said the Baron.

"That'd do it," said Axel.

Welding sparks lit up the Baron's mangled face from below like a Halloween decoration. "They claim to respect me. I am the founder of the Institute, after all. But I sought only to save lives, not to corrupt them. What they have done in my name is ... an **abomination**."

The word *abomination* echoed in Axel's mind. Once again, he wondered what his father would look like if he found him.

"Do you know how to get to the Tower of the Living Computer?" he asked urgently.

"Oh, yes."

"That's where my dad is! So what is it, exactly?"

The Baron was silent for a moment. Axel feared the news was so terrible that the Baron couldn't bring himself to say it.

"The Living Computer is a network made of

human beings," the Baron said, finally. "Each one has a circuit in their head that lets them connect up to other test subjects. Together, the power of their minds forms an organic computer more powerful than any circuit of metal and silicon."

Axel was very still. "You mean he's working for them?"

"Not by choice," the Baron said gently. "They are using him, using the power of his wonderful brain. And it may be dangerous to disconnect him."

Axel felt a lump rising in his throat. "But why him? I know he's clever, but ..."

"Not for his intelligence. For his *imagination*. Your father's mind can create ideas that break new horizons in science."

"AXEL, ARE YOU ALL RIGHT?" BEAST said.

"No," Axel said.

"PLEASE REATTACH MY ARM QUICKLY, BARON. I NEED TO GIVE AXEL A HUG."

"Almost done," the Baron said, squinting at the mess of wires he was working on.

Axel put his tea down, unfinished. "He used to make up stories," he said. "Every night, when I was little. He'd tell me about the adventures we would go on. We'd meet the fat King of the Sun, and his partner, the skinny King of the Moon, and battle the **space eels** for treasure. The forest of silver spiders, and the Pirate Princess, and the **Horrible Fartdragon** of Patagonia ..."

"There is a tissue in the box next to you," the Baron said.

"That's what Dad's imagination is for," Axel said, with hot tears rolling down his cheeks. "They can't have it. I won't let them."

He took a tissue and swabbed his eyes.

"And we are done!" The Baron leaned back, making a noise like bedsprings. "I have fixed the worst damage. Your self-repair systems will take care of the rest."

BEAST flexed his arm and **wiggled** his fingers.

"GOOD AS NEW."

"Baron, will you help me get my father back, please?" Axel said, as BEAST put his arm around him. The robot's arm was heavy but comforting on his shoulders.

"It will be my very great pleasure," said the Baron. "I have not gone on a **wild rampage** for many years now. I think the Neuron Institute ought to be reminded of why they are afraid of me."

CHAPTER 8

Axel shifted BEAST into **GALAHAD**, his sword-and-shield fighting form. They followed the Baron up a spiral staircase that wound around and around.

"This route will lead us right into the Tower of the Living Computer!" the Baron crowed.

"Won't they know we're coming?"

"Ah, they do not know this old castle like I do. It holds so many secrets. The passages, the crypts, the attics, the dungeons below the dungeons. We will be upon them before they know it!"

We're nearly at the final battle, Axel thought. *If this were a game, I'd really want to save my progress in case things went badly. But you can't save your progress in real life. We need to plan, and that means knowing what we're up against. The Baron is strong and brave, but "go crazy and break things" isn't my kind of a plan.*

He asked: "So when you run amok through the castle **smashing** stuff up, what do they try to stop you with?"

"They send their silly little soldiers to fight me," said the Baron. "Cyborg warriors, indeed! **Weaklings.** I shall scatter them like bowling pins and break their tommy guns across my knee!"

Tommy guns? Axel thought. *Aren't they from, like, gangster times?*

"When did you last fight them, out of interest?" he asked casually.

"I forget," the Baron said. "It was a magnificent battle, though. They were taken completely by surprise. When I broke through the wall, they were all watching a man landing on the moon!"

Beast piped up. "SO THAT WAS IN NINETEEN SIXTY –"

"We'd better keep quiet in case they hear us," Axel interrupted, giving BEAST a worried glance.

This isn't going to be as easy as the Baron thinks, he thought. *He hasn't fought the Institute since before Mom was born. They have better weapons than tommy guns now! And that Grabbem angel thing will be out to get us, too.*

The Baron led them down a passageway so narrow they had to walk sideways, and behind the wall of what must have been the bathroom, judging by the noises coming from it.

"Almost there," the Baron whispered. "We will break in to the very room where the Living Computer is kept."

"And I'll **rip** my dad right out of it," Axel promised.

Axel knew they were getting close when he heard the hum of machinery. The Baron grinned and pointed at an oblong sheet of canvas. "Ha! The old 'secret passage covered by a painting' trick! Let us rush them."

"Wait," whispered Axel. "I want to take a look first."

He poked a tiny hole in the painting and peered through.

The chamber was round, with twelve computer terminals spaced evenly around it. Above each one was a platform with a safety rail and a ladder leading up to it, and on each platform stood a white shape like an Egyptian mummy case. Cables connected them together. Gigantic screens high on the walls showed a kaleidoscope of patterns, like atoms joining and joining again in beautiful, complicated combinations. Four scientists in white coats studied the terminals and took notes: one tall, one short, one bearded, and one in little round glasses.

It took Axel's breath away. So much power … and so much evil.

"Some scientists worked to make machines that could think, like our friend BEAST here," whispered the Baron. "But the Neuron Institute saw things the other way around. They wanted to use thinking minds as parts of a machine. You see why I call them **monsters**."

"Those mummy-case things. Are they ..."

"Yes. There are people in there, asleep. One of them is your father."

Axel raised the GALAHAD sword high. "BEAST, it's time to finish this."

"BEAST WILL BE WITH YOU TILL THE END, AXEL."

With a **yell** that shook the tower, Axel **slashed** the painting apart. He strode into the chamber.

Yelling in alarm, the scientists scrambled away from him. The short one ran for a switch on the wall.

"Don't touch that!"

The Baron came sprinting out of the passage, **bellowing** like a bull. He launched himself through the air and slammed the scientist onto his back in a rugby tackle.

"It's the monster!" screamed the scientist with the glasses. "Call Professor Payne, quick!"

"Forget that," snarled the beardy one. "Let's fight him ourselves. Time to put our **cyborg implants** to good use!" He pulled open his shirt. Instead of a pale, hairy chest and belly, Axel saw shiny metal.

"Baron, watch out," he shouted. "They're cyber-enhanced!"

"That's right," the beardy scientist sneered. "We've all got built-in armor and weapons. It's a perk of the job!"

"BEAST IS GLAD," said BEAST bravely.

"Glad? Why?"

"BECAUSE NOW BEAST CAN HIT YOU,

AND NOT FEEL BAD ABOUT IT."

And BEAST bashed him with his shield. The beardy scientist flew across the room, hit the wall like a frog fired from a cannon and slid gently down in a crumpled heap.

"Just shoot them!" yelled the tall scientist, pulling off a rubber glove to reveal a hand made of metal. He jerked his hand forward in a martial arts move, and a crackling ball of blue lightning the size of a football whammed toward BEAST's head.

Axel quickly whacked it aside with the GALAHAD shield. In a **ftazzzm** of sparks, the ball was deflected and went whizzing back into the tall scientist's face. He didn't get out of the way in time and went dancing madly across the floor, howling, as electric arcs *fizzled* across his body.

"Leave these fools to me, my young friend!

Save your father!" roared the Baron, who was still pinning the short scientist to the floor.

The last scientist left standing, the one with the glasses, seemed to be more cowardly than the rest. He had taken cover behind a tray of instruments and was aiming some sort of gun that looked like a trombone with blinking lights all over it.

The Baron flung the short scientist at him, using him as a missile. There was a *howl* and a **crash**, and the pair of them went down in a flailing jumble of arms and legs.

Axel thought quickly. He'd have to use the computers to find out which capsule his dad was in, but that would mean typing on a keyboard. No way would he be able to work those fiddly little keys using BEAST's big robot hands.

He opened BEAST's canopy, jumped out and

ran to the nearest terminal. The displays made no sense to him. What did **AUTO RECT-PURG** mean? It sounded like a laxative. And what about **CEREBRO COND**? It was at seventy percent, whatever it was.

With shaking hands he tapped the screen controls, trying to find something to tell him which container his dad was in.

For once, luck was on his side. He yelled, "Yes!" as the screen flashed up a diagram of the room, complete with the twelve mummy cases. Each one had a nameplate beside it. **SANDERS. CASSERLY. WESTON. PATERSON. BRAYBURN.**

Found him. It was the very one Axel was standing under.

His arms and legs moved in a blur as he climbed up the ladder to reach the container. A cold mist oozed from it.

Panic overtook him as he saw no way to open the smooth, seamless shape. There was a control panel next to it, but it was behind a locked glass case. In desperation, Axel grabbed a wrench from the floor and **smashed** the glass.

Alarms blared. The lights in the room flashed orange. "CONTAINMENT BREACH," thundered an electronic voice. "EMERGENCY. DEPLOYING RESERVE FORCES."

Axel didn't have time to worry about those. He jabbed the door control with his thumb.

The container slowly opened like a vampire's coffin, releasing a cloud of white vapor. And Axel stared and stared at what lay there in front of him.

CHAPTER 9

"Dad! Wake up!"

A memory flashed into Axel's mind. *Dad's birthday. I was four. I went and jumped up and down on the bed to wake him up. It was still dark outside. But he wasn't even angry. He laughed ...*

His dad was lying there, still as a statue, his face peaceful. Thick cables were plugged into a socket in the back of his neck. Axel reached to pull them out, then hesitated. The Baron had said it was **dangerous** to disconnect him. What if something went wrong?

As if that wasn't bad enough, the fight down in the chamber below him was far from over. The emergency system had summoned backup – and now it was here.

The main door opened and there stood two frightful figures, bulky as quarterbacks

and **ugly as burst garbage bags**. They were like men stuffed into oversized muscle suits made from steel and rubber. One was covered with crackling ice crystals that kept growing over his body and falling off. Pipes filled with swirling white gas stuck out from his back. The next warrior had two saw blades on his arms that looked like they'd been ripped off some piece of farming equipment. They glowed as red as swords in a blacksmith's forge.

"WarBorgs reporting in!" they roared together.

"IceBorg!" yelled the first.

"BlazeBorg!" boomed the second.

"And the two of us are going to take you down!" they finished.

"AXEL?" stammered BEAST.

The two WarBorgs stomped forward.

The Baron put his arm around BEAST's shoulder. "Come, my metal brother. Let us stand firm like a wall of iron, and protect young Axel together!"

"BEAST IS READY," said BEAST, not sounding ready at all.

Axel wanted to help BEAST, but he couldn't do anything from up here on the platform. He touched his dad's cool, calm face. "Wake up, Dad," he begged. "Please tell me what I need to do."

But his dad said nothing. He lay still and silent.

The WarBorgs chose their targets. IceBorg growled low and faced the Baron. BlazeBorg scraped his blades together, sending hot sparks showering down, and advanced on BEAST.

"Here they come," the Baron boomed. "Brace yourself!"

IceBorg lowered his head. A sheet of ice began to spread out under his feet. He launched himself into a charge and went *skidding* across the room, gliding on the ice he created, picking up speed as he went, like a hockey player. He **slammed** into the Baron, nearly knocking him off his feet.

"Oof!" the Baron gasped.

IceBorg's thick arms locked around the Baron's waist and they struggled together like wrestlers in a ring. Where IceBorg's hands gripped the Baron's body, patches of frost began to appear, turning his flesh blue-white.

"Is that the best you can do?" the Baron grunted.

IceBorg laughed. "You're just an old machine, not a slick new model like me! Old machines seize up in the cold. In a minute, you won't be able to move!"

Sure enough, the Baron was slowing down. He beat his fists on IceBorg's back, but the WarBorg held on with grim strength. He just couldn't break that grip.

BEAST was having an even worse time. BlazeBorg lashed out at him, striking him with one blade after the other.

BEAST couldn't get a single attack in. He huddled behind the GALAHAD shield, doing his best to protect himself. The red-hot blades **clanged** and *sizzled* against the shield's metal. It was like trying to fight a kitchen blender! BEAST parried the blades as best he could, but one of them struck his chest above the letter B and left a smoking black mark.

"AXEL?" he howled. "I DON'T KNOW WHAT TO DO!"

On a screen above Axel, Professor Payne's gloating face appeared.

"What a touching family reunion. It is a shame your father will never leave this building."

"I'll unplug him right now!" Axel yelled.

"Will you? When the Living Computer is the only thing keeping him alive?"

Axel didn't know whether to believe the professor or not. He could be lying. But what if he wasn't?

The Baron groaned. His limbs creaked in IceBorg's grasp like an old battleship being battered by a storm. Half his body was covered in ice now, and one of his legs was frozen to the spot, but he was still standing.

BEAST could do nothing but keep moving back, away from BlazeBorg's **whirling** blades.

The WarBorgs were going to win, and they knew it. It was just a matter of time before they wore the Baron and BEAST down.

BEAST thought: *I CANNOT WIN WITHOUT AXEL'S HELP!*

Then he thought: *BUT I HAVE TO. I HAVE TO BE BRAVE. THINK! WHAT WOULD AXEL DO? AXEL IS A GAMER. IF THIS FIGHT WAS IN A GAME, HOW WOULD AXEL WIN?*

BEAST's memory banks hastily shuffled through all the games he had seen Axel play.

In multiplayer games, you could often choose a role. Tank classes were slow moving and could take hits, but didn't do major damage. Rogue classes were fast moving and did heavy damage. The trick to winning a fight was to have a mix of classes on your team ...

The Baron was slow moving and tough. In his GALAHAD form, BEAST was also slow moving and tough.

BEAST thought: *WE HAVE BOTH PICKED TANK! I NEED TO BE A ROGUE!*

"SHIFTING FORM TO **SHADO!**" he announced. SHADO was his panther-like stealth striker form, equipped with powerful claws and fast movement. It took only a second for BEAST's form to change.

"Shapeshifting? That trick won't save you," snarled BlazeBorg.

He swung at SHADO, but the transformed robot moved as quickly as a cat, leaping out of the blade's path and **bounding** around to the side.

Before BlazeBorg could work out where he had gone, SHADO had already prepared his next attack. The Baron and IceBorg were still locked in a grapple – and IceBorg's back was exposed.

SHADO pounced. IceBorg **shrieked** as SHADO's claws sliced through the cables and pipes that protruded from his back. Freezing gas fountained out, and in seconds the mighty IceBorg was a crumpled heap on the floor. He looked like a dismal damp rag.

"Bro," he gasped feebly. "Avenge me, bro!"

BlazeBorg turned around. He saw that IceBorg had fallen, and howled, "Noooo!"

The Baron shook fragments of ice from his body and beckoned BlazeBorg over. "What are you waiting for? Attack me, if you dare!"

BlazeBorg let out a furious yell and charged, just as the Baron had meant him to. While he was paying attention to the Baron, he didn't even notice SHADO had crept away into hiding, ready for another strike.

BlazeBorg raised his mighty blades. "I'm going to rip you to pieces!" he roared.

"Go ahead and try!" the Baron roared back, and raised his fists.

From the darkness at the edge of the room, SHADO pounced. He clung to BlazeBorg's back just like the jungle cat he looked like. BlazeBorg shrieked and threw up his arms – and the Baron quickly knocked him **sprawling** with a single punch. He fell to the ground and didn't get back up.

"Good kitty," he chuckled, and gave SHADO a pat on the head. "Not very bright, these WarBorgs, eh?"

Meanwhile Axel stood beside his dad, still wrestling with his **impossible** decision. If he didn't unplug his dad, he would never be able to save him. But if he *did*, his dad might die.

His hand hovered over the plug. He couldn't risk it.

Crying inside, Axel reached up to press the switch and close his father's capsule again. At least this way he was safe.

His thumb rested on the switch ...

And he stopped.

"No, I'll find a way," he said. "No matter what."

No more hesitation. Axel pulled the plugs out.

His dad gave a sudden **gasp**. His body **shook**. And his eyes **flew** open.

"Axel?" The voice was hoarse, as if it hadn't been used in a long time. "I called to you. I thought it was a dream ..."

Axel fought back tears. "I'm here, Dad.

It's okay. You're safe!"

He held his dad in his arms. They hugged for a long time. Neither one wanted to let go.

The Baron cheered. "Bravo, young man. Great deeds have been done here today!"

His dad's eyes widened. "Who's that? And the robot?"

"The Baron's my friend," Axel said, "and BEAST's my *best* friend. I've got so much to tell you. I can't wait!"

BEAST changed back into his regular form and clapped his metal hands. "BEAST IS SO HAPPY," he said. "CAN WE GO HOME NOW, AXEL?"

But BlazeBorg had only been **stunned**, and had gotten to his feet again. Nobody saw him until it was too late. He thrust one of his blades right into BEAST's body. It burst out the other side.

BEAST fell to his knees and toppled slowly forward.

Axel screamed, "No!"

"POWER CORE DESTROYED," whispered BEAST. "GOODBYE."

And his eyes went dark.

CHAPTER 10

Axel, his dad, and the Baron looked down at BEAST with horror. BlazeBorg looked up at them with a wide smirk of **victory** on his face.

Axel's dad stepped out of the capsule, pale and shaking. His legs **buckled** under him, weak from so many months in hibernation, and he grabbed the safety rail to steady himself.

Axel just stared. It had happened so quickly.

"He's gone," he whispered. "I can't believe it. How can BEAST be gone?"

The next moment, the robotic angel with the demon face strode into the room.

"Huh. Looks like I missed all the **action**. Too bad."

(Hundreds of miles away, in the tank of bubbly liquid where he hung suspended, Gus Grabbem Junior was grinning. Axel was *finally* going to lose.)

"Excellent," said Professor Payne from the screen. "BlazeBorg, return the test subject to his capsule immediately."

"And the boy?" growled BlazeBorg.

"Give him to our Grabbem friend. I believe there is a long-standing score to settle!"

BlazeBorg started toward Axel and his dad, but the Baron moved to block his path. "Another step, and I'll **destroy** you!" he roared.

The robotic angel stepped over BEAST, who lay motionless on the floor with smoke pouring out of him. It stood face-to-face with the Baron.

"You fight pretty good for an old guy," it said. "But you're still going down."

A blue field of energy *fizzed* around the angel's fist. The angel struck the Baron one devastating blow under the chin. His head rocked back and he fell, collapsing in slow motion like a demolished factory chimney.

"You're all clear. Stuff that guy back in his freezer," the angel told BlazeBorg.

BlazeBorg climbed up the ladder to where Axel and his father were, and the mean look on his face reminded Axel of the *snarling* cyberwolves in the forest.

The whole mission had been for nothing. Axel felt like his heart had been ripped in half.

He hugged his dad tight as BlazeBorg reached for him.

"You lose," the angel said.

Axel's dad let go of Axel, stepped forward on unsteady legs and faced BlazeBorg. He raised his **trembling** fists. "No. I won't let you."

"Dad!" Axel screamed.

"Axel, get behind me. I'll stop them!"

"You don't stand a chance against me," BlazeBorg growled. "You've got no weapons!"

Axel's dad laughed. "I don't care. I'll still fight you with every breath in my body."

"Wait," interrupted the robotic angel. "You'd ... you'd do that? Why?"

"Don't you get it? I'm his dad. That's what dads *do*."

"Don't lie!" the angel rasped.

The look Axel's father gave the robotic angel was terrible. (It seemed to penetrate right into

Gus's soul. He shuddered in his tank.)

Axel's dad said, "Any man worth calling a man would do the same for his son. Does a **metal creep** like you even know what a father is?"

"Shut up and come with us," grunted BlazeBorg. And he reached out to grab Axel's dad.

But something was happening just then. Something nobody could have predicted.

Deep in the messed-up closet of Gus Grabbem Junior's mind, a light bulb had suddenly gone on.

Any man worth calling a man would do the same for his son.

For as long as Gus could remember, he had been **angry**. He loved to break things. All his life, there had been things to break. Because his dad had bought him things.

A memory flashed into his mind. He saw his own father, the famous billionaire, sitting at his desk. *I was only four years old.*

Dad? Play with me, Dad? Please?

Can't, son. Too busy. Tell you what. I'll buy you the biggest train set any boy ever had. You can go play with that, eh? Good lad.

The train set had filled a room of the house. Gus remembered standing there, all alone, surrounded by his expensive present. He had spent the afternoon running the trains into one another, **stamping** on them and **_throwing_** them at the wall.

The next day, all the broken trains had been silently replaced.

Too busy.

Got business to do.

Go play in your room.

He remembered his mother saying, "Goodness knows your father and I buy you enough stuff."

They gave me THINGS. They expected me to be happy with THINGS. Because neither of them cared about ME! They never had the time for their own son! I was supposed to play with the stuff they bought me, by myself, like a good *boy – but all I ever wanted was to play with THEM. My parents.*

No wonder he'd **smashed** the stuff they bought him. It meant nothing. But an hour of their time – just an hour – that would have meant everything.

He looked at Axel's father standing between his son and BlazeBorg. He saw something he had never had.

And for the first time in his life, Gus understood where he had gone wrong.

I never wanted things, he realized. *I just wanted my dad.*

Axel watched the robotic angel raise its blaster arm and take careful aim. He braced himself for the end.

But the angel didn't blast him. It blasted BlazeBorg.

A lance of brilliant light **speared** through the WarBorg's arm, slicing his blade clean off. BlazeBorg held up the stump and looked at it blankly.

"What are you doing?" Professor Payne screamed from the screen. "Your aim is off! You hit my WarBorg!"

The angel said nothing. It dialed the power up to a higher setting, aimed and fired again.

This time, BlazeBorg was blown clean through the wall. He fell with a sound like a trash can full of scrap metal being emptied out of a window.

"No!" screeched the professor. "Grabbem will answer for this! You will –"

"Oh, shut up," the angel said, and shot the screen.

There was silence for a moment.

Axel couldn't believe what he was seeing. "Did you do that on purpose?"

"Yeah."

"So ... did you ... did you just **change sides?**"

The angel didn't answer for a long time. Then it spread its shining silver wings. "There's still eleven other people stuck in those capsules. Get them all out."

"Okay," said Axel. "But how are we going to fly them out of here? The turrets will shoot down anyone who comes close!"

"I'll take care of the turrets," the angel said.

Then it flew out through the hole in the wall, leaving Axel speechless.

Out in the forest of Eisenbern, Agent Omega had finished repairing the crashed MOT-BOL. Now he was watching the tower tops of the castle in amazement. The robotic angel was destroying the Neuron Institute's weapons.

"I thought that angel was with Grabbem?" he said aloud. "This doesn't make any sense!"

The angel had just flown straight through one of the gun turrets like a **missile**. It flew on to the next without even slowing down. Fireballs blossomed in the sky, lighting up the castle like victory fireworks.

One by one, the gun turrets were blown to bits. The angel soared above them like a rejoicing spirit, reborn in the fire.

"Looks like I'm clear to go fetch Axel," Omega said. "Hey! Whoever's flying that thing, thanks!"

When Gus piloted the robotic angel back inside the Tower of the Living Computer, he found a crowd waiting for him. All the people who had been imprisoned inside their capsules were free. They were gathered in a circle around BEAST, who was lying still. The Baron, who had woken up, plugged a power cable into him.

BEAST's eyes lit up with a feeble **glimmer**. "AXEL. ARE YOU THERE?"

Axel took his hand. "I'm here. You're going to be fine."

"NO. BEAST IS FINISHED. THERE IS ONLY ONE THING LEFT TO DO."

"Don't talk like that."

"THIS PLACE MUST BE DESTROYED."

"Stop it!" Axel demanded.

"ACTIVATING **PHOENIX** APP."

"Don't. You'll die!"

"BEAST INITIATING SELF-DESTRUCT SEQUENCE. OVERLOADING POWER CORE NOW …"

CHAPTER 11

BEAST beeped.

"ERROR. POWER CORE NOT FOUND. PHOENIX APP HAS CRASHED."

"**Crashed?**" Axel said. That had never happened before.

The robotic angel laughed. "Dude. I don't want to spoil your big moment, but how were you going to overload your power core when that WarBorg already destroyed it?"

Axel looked at the hole in BEAST's body, and almost wept with relief. "He's right!"

BEAST's eyes turned bright pink.

"BEAST IS VERY EMBARRASSED," he muttered.

Axel hugged him. "Don't be."

"BUT BEAST WAS GOING TO DO A BIG NOBLE SELF-SACRIFICE! AND YOU WOULD REMEMBER BEAST AND BE SAD BUT HAPPY BECAUSE WE HAD HAD ADVENTURES. AND YOU WOULD SAY 'POOR OLD BEAST BUT NEVER MIND THE FAMILY IS BACK TOGETHER NOW AND WE DID NOT NEED HIM REALLY.'"

Axel's dad knelt by BEAST's side. "Is that what this is about?"

"MAYBE."

"Don't be silly, **big guy**. There'll always be a place for Axel's best friend in this family."

Axel stood and looked up at the robotic angel. The face still looked **terrifying**, but something about the eyes seemed much more human now.

"I was sure I knew who you were," he said. "But now I'm not so sure."

"Listen," said the angel, pointing to itself. "This thing's going to shut down any moment. There's a brand-new, juiced-up Grabbem power core in it. Take it out and stick it in your robot." The angel wrenched open a panel in its chest, and pulled out a mass of cables.

Axel saw the power core, pulsing with light in the midst of them.

"Thanks." He reached out to grasp it.

"Any time … **noob**."

Axel's eyes widened. "Hey, wait a minute!"

But Axel could tell whoever was controlling the angel couldn't hear him anymore. The connection was broken. It was a lifeless piece of machinery now.

He closed his fingers around the power core and pulled.

"What were you thinking, Gus?"

Two burly technicians hauled Gus Grabbem Junior out of the control tank. His mother stood by, wrestling with the cap on a bottle of migraine pills, while Mr. Grabbem folded his arms and shouted at his son.

"That project cost a **fortune!** I've got Professor Payne threatening to break off our partnership! You are in deep trouble this time, young man. Don't expect any more presents!"

A doctor shone a light into Gus's eyes, prodded his arm and made notes on a tablet.

"You were in there for a long time, sonny. How do you feel?"

Gus thought about it.

"I feel … *good,*" he said.

Not long after, the MOT-BOL prepared to lift off from what was left of the Neuron Institute. The little craft had never felt so crowded. All the people who had been trapped inside the Living Computer were **crammed** inside, along with Axel, his dad and Agent Omega, who was handing out drinks for the journey.

"Do you have an airsick bag, please?" asked Mr. Paterson, who had been in the capsule next to Axel's dad. "Air travel makes me queasy."

"Use the floor," snapped Agent Omega. "I was not cut out to be a flight attendant," he grumbled to himself. "Everyone, fasten your seat belts. We are getting out of here."

"And I think I speak for all of us when I say thanks for the ride!" said Axel's dad.

"You're very welcome," said Omega, sounding less grumpy.

BEAST hung in his special docking frame, deep in robot hibernation. His damaged systems were slowly repairing themselves, drawing on what little power the MOT-BOL could spare. Axel sat beside him, holding on his lap the power core they'd taken from the angel. It was surprisingly small, about the size of a grapefruit.

Like a heart, Axel thought. *Who would have thought there was a good heart deep down inside something that seemed so evil?*

"He's going to be okay, you know," Axel's dad said.

"I know," said Axel.

"Your mom will help get that core installed, once he's ready. She's the best mechanic in the world."

"Here we go!" Agent Omega said, and started the engines.

The MOT-BOL **wobbled unsteadily** up into the air. It kept climbing, and the castle below gradually shrank into the distance.

Axel's dad hugged him tight. "I can't believe it. I'm going home. And it's all thanks to you. I couldn't be more proud."

It was a warm October evening, two weeks later.

Dinner was over, the plates cleared away, and the family sat in the backyard watching the stars. Matt Brayburn lay on the grass, and Nedra was curled up with her head on his chest. Axel sat nearby. This all felt perfectly normal, and yet too good to be true. Things were finally back the way they ought to be.

"Welcome home, **big fella**," Nedra said, and smiled.

"It's never going to get old, is it?" Matt said. "You saying that, and me hearing it?"

"Never."

Axel smiled to himself. He stood up and stretched. "I'm heading indoors for a bit."

"Don't bother to do the dishes," Nedra said. "They can wait till morning."

On his way into the house, Axel passed Rosie and Agent Omega, who were sitting on lawn chairs and inventing new constellations. The pair of them had been spending a lot of time together lately. Now that he didn't have to work at Grabbem anymore, Omega had lightened up a *lot*.

"That's the toilet plunger," said Rosie. "See those three stars? They're the handle."

"And that cluster, with the bright one right at the top? That's the One-Legged Wombat," said Omega.

"Blimey, so it is. But what are those stars next to him, then?"

"He's playing a saxophone, *obviously*," Omega said, deadly serious. Then they both cracked up.

Axel slipped into the darkened kitchen. He expected to find BEAST in there, being a refrigerator. After all the excitement of going on missions and shifting into different forms, BEAST sometimes liked to turn into a fridge and just – as Axel liked to say – **chill out**. After all he'd been through, nobody blamed him for wanting to take it easy for a while.

But BEAST wasn't being a fridge tonight. He was looking out the window at the night sky, stargazing like everyone else in the family.

"You okay?" Axel asked.

"OH, YES. BEAST IS FINE!"

"How's the new power core working out?"

BEAST sighed contentedly. "IT IS SO GOOD. I HAVE LOTS OF ENERGY, AXEL. IT IS MAKING ME A BIT FIDGETY. I THINK I SHOULD BE DOING MORE WITH IT."

"Don't feel like being a fridge tonight, huh?"

"THE MOON LOOKS NICE," said BEAST. "I WONDER IF I WILL EVER GO THERE."

Axel laughed. "Maybe we will."

He left BEAST to his daydreams of **space travel** and opened the door to his room.

He took his old game console from under the bed and started it up. For some reason, he had the urge to play *Tankinator Arena*. He hadn't played it in months. As the screens flashed up, he saw everything was exactly as he'd left it. AX-MAN still had great scores, but none of the good Tankinators you had to pay real money for. Oh well, he'd always thought skill was more important than money anyway.

He put his headset on and got ready to find a match. "Let's see. Who else is online …"

A message flashed up on his screen. **INCOMING TEAM INVITE: BAGGER_63.**

Axel looked at that name, and slowly grinned. Fighting on the same side? That wasn't something he could ever have expected.

A familiar voice spoke in his headphones:

"Well, noob? You want to team up or what?"

Axel thought for a moment, then clicked on ACCEPT.

"Let's play," he said.

THE END

ABOUT THE AUTHOR
& ILLUSTRATOR

ADRIAN C. BOTT

is a gamer, writer and professional adventure creator. He lives in Sussex, England, with his family and is allowed to play video games whenever he wants.

ANDY ISAAC lives in Melbourne, Australia. He discovered his love of illustration through comic books when he was eight years old, and has been creating his own characters ever since.

AXEL & BEAST

THE GRABBEM GETAWAY

ADRIAN C. BOTT ART BY ANDY ISAAC

AXEL & BEAST

ANTARCTIC ATTACK

ADRIAN C. BOTT ART BY ANDY ISAAC

AXEL & BEAST

TROPICAL TANGLE

ADRIAN C. BOTT ART BY ANDY ISAAC

AXEL & BEAST

ROBOTIC RUMBLE

ADRIAN C. BOTT ART BY ANDY ISAAC

AXEL & BEAST

THE OMEGA OPERATION

ADRIAN C. BOTT ART BY ANDY ISAAC

AXEL & BEAST

CASTLE OF CYBORGS

ADRIAN C. BOTT ART BY ANDY ISAAC

ACKNOWLEDGEMENTS
FROM THE AUTHOR

Massive thanks to everyone at HGE, especially Penny, Haylee, Luna and of course the incomparable Marisa, who started it all. Cheers and fist bumps to Andy, companion on this adventure, who brought everything to such wonderful life. And all my love to Lucy and Sabrina for keeping me going from day to day.